1295

BRENDAN, MORGAN AND THE BEST EVER CLOUD MACHINE

Design and graphic realization
Helmut Weyerstrahs

Annick Press gratefully acknowledges the
contributions of The Canada Council and
The Ontario Arts Council

Canadian Cataloguing in Publication Data

Evans, Gerrem.
   Brendan, Morgan and the best ever cloud machine

ISBN 0-920303-18-8 (bound)   0-920303-17-X (pbk.)

I. Ritchie, Scot.   II. Title.

PS8559.V35B74 1985   jC813'.54   C84-099774-4
PZ7.E93Br 1985

Distributed in Canada and the USA by:
Firefly Books Ltd.
3520 Pharmacy Avenue, Unit 1c
Scarborough, Ontario
M1W 2T8

Printed and bound in Canada
by Johanns Graphics, Waterloo, Ontario

Brendan, Morgan and the Best Ever Cloud Machine

Story
Gerrem Evans

Art
Scot Ritchie

ANNICK PRESS LTD., Toronto, Canada M2N 5S3

One sunny morning Brendan and Morgan watched a cloud drifting above them in the sky. They watched it change shape from a ball to a fish to a horse.

Brendan decided he wanted to be like a cloud, to change shape and float over mountains and rivers and see wonderful things on land and sea.

"But," Brendan said to himself, "clouds don't have bones. How can I be like a cloud if I have bones?"

"Morgan," he said to his little brother, "look like you don't have bones," and Morgan obligingly collapsed to the ground.

Morgan practised
being as quiet as a cloud

while Brendan frowned

and thought

and pondered

and speculated.

4

Then Brendan formed a plan. He wanted a cloud that would fly. It had to look like a cloud outside and have a machine inside, so he could sit and control the cloud's movements. He wanted it to go up and down, and left and right.

First, he found a bench and a platform to put the bench on.

"Morgan," Brendan asked, "help me. Go up the hill and catch a cloud. I want to see what it looks like up close."

Morgan ran off to catch a cloud.

Then, after Brendan had hammered and sawed and nailed and glued most of the cloud-machine together, Morgan came back with a sad face and an empty pot.

"Never mind, Morgan, you can do something else."

6

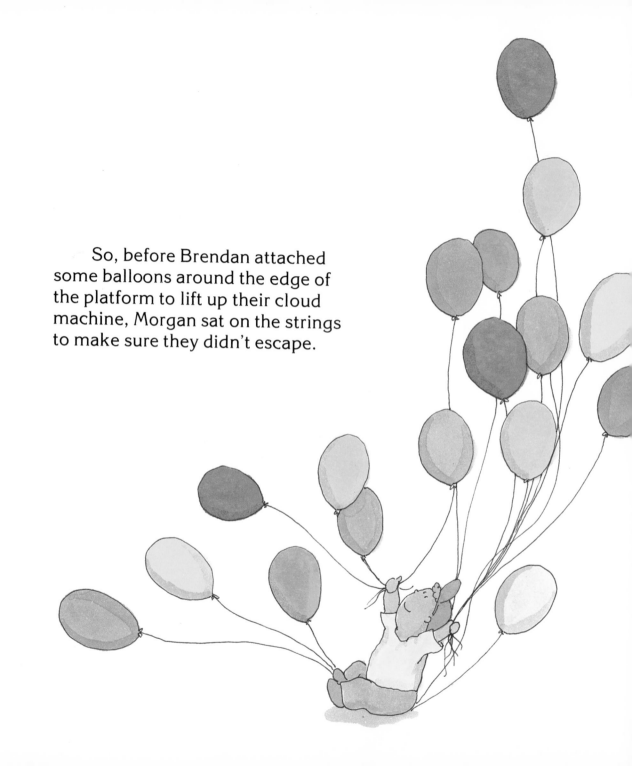

So, before Brendan attached
some balloons around the edge of
the platform to lift up their cloud
machine, Morgan sat on the strings
to make sure they didn't escape.

7

Then Brendan made some squirters. The squirters would control the shape of the cloud. The hot air squirters would make the cloud bigger and the cold air squirters would make the cloud smaller.

Soon they were ready to climb aboard. And up they zoomed, up up up up up
Trees flew by. Birds stopped in mid-air squawking and flapping. Brendan grinned, held his breath and concentrated on the squirters. Morgan gasped and laughed and hung on to his seat belt.

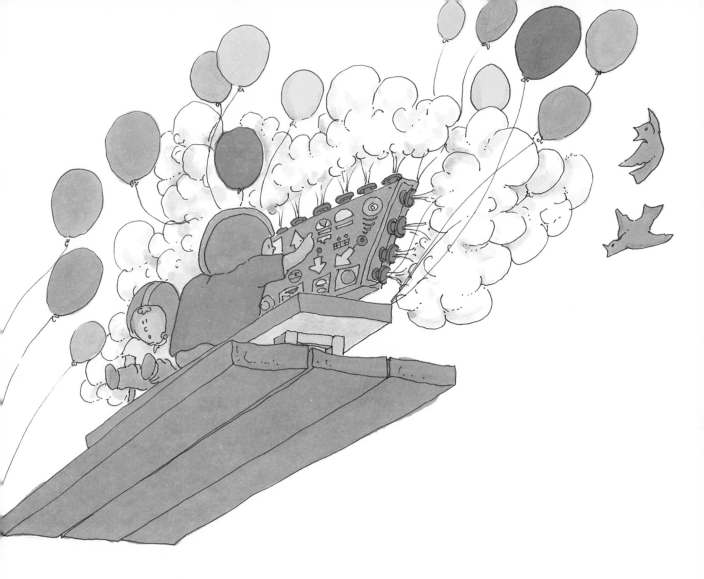

There was a lurch and a slide.

12

Then everything jumped and bumped and began to wobble. It was a jerky, lumpy wobble. Somehow the button controls didn't work very well. The wind was too strong and pushed the platform right when Brendan wanted to go left and straight ahead when he wanted to go back.

Brendan pushed buttons and squished squirters until his face was red. He had a lopsided cloud going nowhere.

Down they came very fast and very bumpily.

14

Brendan sat and he frowned. Morgan lay beside him, closed one eye and rested just a little bit.

Brendan thought and he pondered and he speculated. At last he had an idea. He needed a sail.

He borrowed a sheet from his bed, found a pole for a mast and fastened it beside the bench on the platform.

"Come on Morgan, let's go."

Morgan opened his eye, stared for a moment at the sky, then pointed.

"Yes, I see it, that black thing. But there aren't any clouds. We'll have the whole sky to ourselves."

They clambered onto the platform.
Brendan pushed the UP button
and off they zoomed again, up up up.

He set the sail and pushed his buttons and squished his squirters. Brendan zigged and Morgan zagged as they flew around the sky. Brendan squished the hot steamy air and Morgan squished the cold icy air. And between them they created a <u>magnificent</u> cloud.

But on one of the zags, Morgan grabbed his brother's arm and pointed over his shoulder.

Looming, and rushing toward them from behind, was a huge, black machine. Brendan saw the printed words, "DIRIGIBLE — CLOUD DISPERSER". He jabbed the UP button and shouted. "Morgan get down!"

They saw spurts of orangy yellow,
like liquid sun rays,
evaporate part of their cloud.

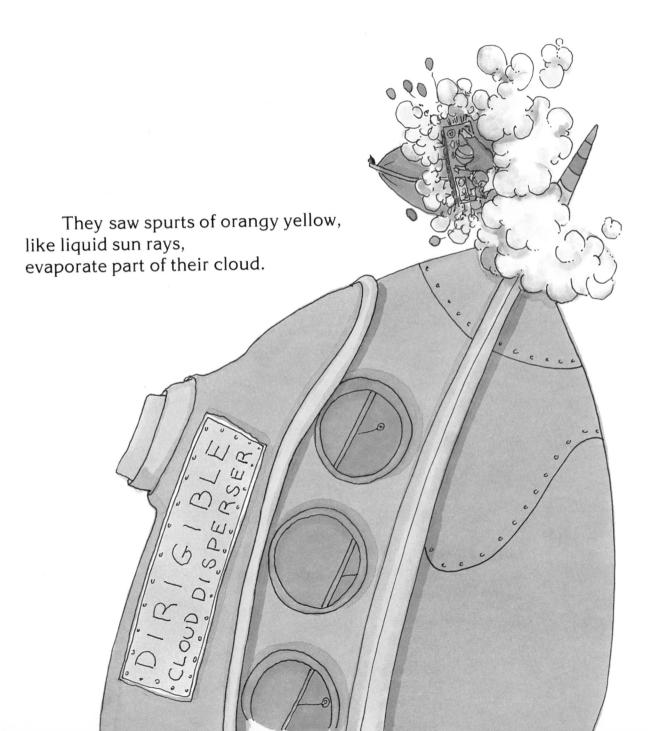

There was a crash as the nose of the Dirigible butted under the platform of the Cloud Machine. They slithered and slid, then wedged against a funnel on top of the Dirigible.

The sail was askew, the mast atilt. Morgan's seat was broken. He closed his eyes and bellowed, "I want to go home. Now."

Brendan peered carefully over the edge. He put his arm around Morgan's shoulders. "Don't worry. Don't worry, we just have to fix a few things." "You sit on the funnel and hang on to the Cloud Machine while I see if the squirters work."

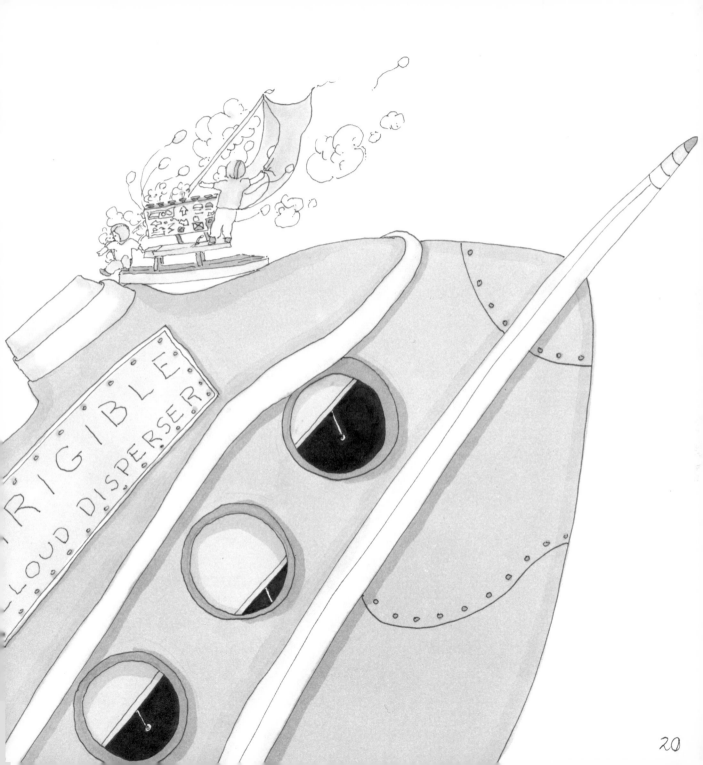

20

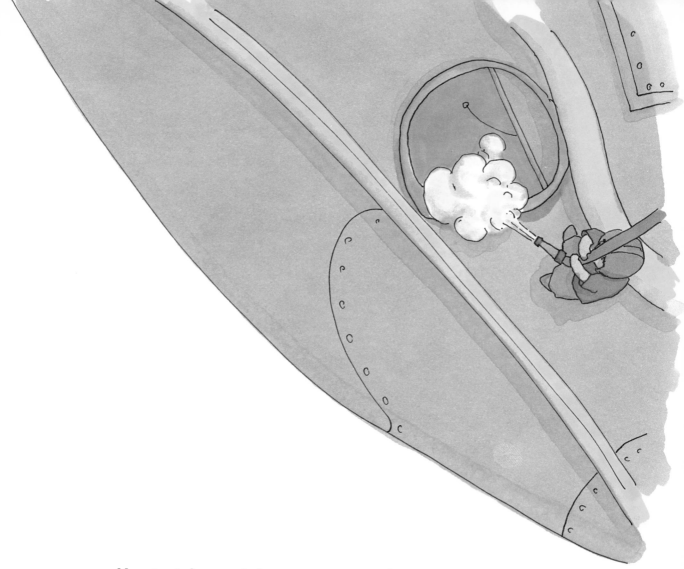

He straightened the mast, re-set the sail, roped the seat together and checked the squirters. The balloons were intact. Then he aimed the hot steamy squirters at the port holes on both sides of the Dirigible. The portholes fogged over. No one could see out and the Dirigible pointed toward the earth.

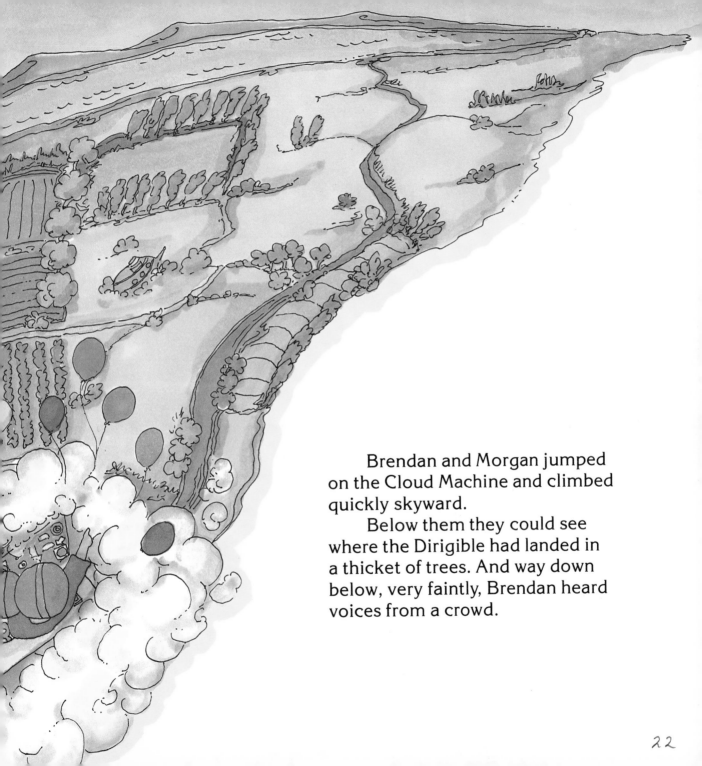

Brendan and Morgan jumped on the Cloud Machine and climbed quickly skyward.

Below them they could see where the Dirigible had landed in a thicket of trees. And way down below, very faintly, Brendan heard voices from a crowd.

"Is it a cloud?"
"Is it a Martian ship?"
"Maybe it's a magic cloud."
"Oh me, oh my, what a peculiar cloud."
"Who could make such a marvellous cloud?"

And away up there, Brendan shouted,
"Me! Me! I did. I did. Me and Morgan did."

They waved to the people below. Brendan grinned at his brother and said, "Did you notice, we are the only cloud in the sky? We have the best ever cloud. And we can go home now if you want."

Morgan nodded.

"What do you want to do after dinner," asked Brendan.
"Dunno," Morgan said.
"Let's build a submarine!"

27